Rusty'S MountaiN

By: DOUGLAS GRIFFETH

ISBN: 978-1-7776021-1-6

Graphic Project: Natalia Junqueira - Dawn Book Design

I have been inspired by many over the years: musicians, mentors, my "mirrors," my family, and of late, myself; however, at this juncture of my journey, none more so than Roxanna, to whom I dedicate this story.

Thank you and love to you all.

Danette

Thank you for your support in
getting Rusty's Mountain
released into the wild.

My hope is that your life,
in some way, has been
enriched through the
experience.

Peace
Doug :)

My passion lives in writing
I live where my passion writes

~ Douglas

Out of Here

I hate homework. Rusty stews over correcting the day's quiz on the bench by the huge bush along the castle wall.

A butterfly flutters through his line of sight. The distraction causes him to chase after it, keen on today being the day he will finally catch a pet. Dodging the dead bushes and flowerbeds overrun with weeds, his stabbing grasps miss the target as it flitters about the unoccupied courtyard. The harder he tries, the more elusive is the butterfly.

"Rusty...you better not be chasing butterflies again!" His female oppressor's crotchety voice reverberates around the sinister, yellow-grey walls.

Cringing dead in his tracks mid-courtyard, he plunks down in despair onto the cracked rim of a decrepit fountain. Its weather-beaten statue centrepiece towers behind him. The face of the barely discernible person is mostly missing, as is the arm that once held what is left of a large urn. No water comes from its pour.

With head hung, he stares at the weeds cropping up between the cobblestones under foot.

Being lonely sucks; I wish I had somebody to hang around with.

"Ah, who needs you anyway," he growls, walking to the staircase leading up to the rampart.

Each stone step receives a stomping foot on the word engraved in it: *worthless, unwanted, inadequate, insignificant, desperate, resentful, lonely, hatred, and shame.*

A castle guard is shaking his fist in the air on approach and screaming, "I hate you! I hate you! I...hate you!"

The beret cinched down over his right ear tops a uniform decorated in the rank of Major and bearing the name flash, *Rajor.*

The angry-looking guard's solid, muscular frame, looming nearly seven feet tall, stops abruptly upon encountering Rusty blocking his path.

"You? Again? Get out of my way!" he says, pushing past to continue his march.

Rusty tags along being respectful yet somewhat defiant of the familiar imposing figure.

"Protecting the castle on your patrol again, Major?"

"Somebody has to protect this dump from the outside world!"

"What's it like in the outside world? I hear things, but I never know if they're true. You've been out there. What's it like? Come on, Major, what's the truth...really?"

Major halts. "You think you can handle the truth?! All right...there's nothin' but heartache out there. Women, they're the enemy. They'll neglect you and reject you when you need 'em the most. They could care less about your needs. They're nothin' but C.N.T.'s: cruel, narcissistic, terrorists. I hate all of 'em!"

"Are you afraid of them like me, Major?"

"Afraid? Of women...? Well, I used to be afraid of 'em, terrified, in fact. But not now. Now I'm afraid of me 'cause of what I want to do to 'em." An evil grin consumes his being. "I want to grab 'em and punch 'em and throw 'em to the ground and kick 'em! Ya, then I'm gonna—."

"Why would you hurt them, Major?"

"You don't know spit, boy. Quit wastin' my time."

Thrusting the pest against the wall, he marches on with his patrol, fist punched in the air and screaming, "I hate you...all of you...you..." as his voice trails off with his disappearance.

Rusty discounts the guard with a wave-off. *What truth is this?*

Looking out from the battlements lining the top of the walls, he spies a gopher in the field beyond.

What a pathetic creature. Every day it's the same, afraid of its own shadow; always so cautious coming out of its hole and constantly looking around in fear, and then bolting back down in an instant for no reason. If I was out there, free, like it is, I certainly wouldn't hide underground, paranoid of the world outside. I'd find the truth, if only I was out there.

His gaze drifts to the horizon. There, on another mountain far in the distance, is a castle, its white walls and golden spires glistening in the bright sun. *How amazing it must be over there. I bet people are free and there are others I can hang with for as long as I want. I would be loved there. One day I am going to live on that mountain, in that castle: the Castle of Love.*

"Rusty! You better not be up on that wall again."

Spanked by her crotchety voice, he descends, snarling a letter on each step, "C-N-T, C-N-T, C-N-T."

A heavy thud coming from behind a thick bramble bush at the base of the stairs accompanies his foot landing off the last step.

Startled, he stops to listen, but there is only silence. Curiosity compels him to investigate.

Gingerly pulling his way in behind stabbing branch barbs, he finds a sinkhole under one of the wall's massive foundation stones. As wide and deep as he is tall, the attraction invites a jump in.

He is surprised to find a tunnel running from under the courtyard on the one side branching outward in several directions beyond the wall on the other.

Looking up to no one watching, he hoots, "I'm out of here!" while ducking to enter one of the tunnels.

Knowingly
Knowing

Crawling through the musty narrow confines of a pitch-black, cramped passage, Rusty touches a junction.

Not another fork. There's no getting out. I am going to die!

His bridled panic chooses a direction and continues the crawl.

"Finally, light!" He scrambles out, able to stand in the dome-like enclosure. Light beams onto his feet through a roughly rounded opening up in the tightly woven tree roots arcing randomly down around him into the dirt. A sizable pile of small bones and fur remnants sits to one side.

Climbing into the light, he finds himself amidst thick brush at the base of a gigantic old-growth evergreen in a thick forest. The air's scent is fresh; its dampness chilly. A pathway beckons a few steps down a slope, past a couple more equally large trees.

Where am I?

Surveying the surroundings, it strikes him. Doing a happy dance, he opens his arms wide and yells to the sky, "I'm free!"

A weasel darting from the opposite side of the tree toward the opening stops abruptly in front of the excited figure. Dropping the dead mouse clenched in its mouth, the critter stands on hind legs. Sniffing the air, whiskers twitch on the end of its long, slender nose as big, round ears wiggle. Inquisitive black eyes probe the suspect up and down.

"Not my fault." The weasel's paws tap its chest before being held up in a defensive posture.

A wide-eyed Rusty gapes at the talking creature and he attempts a tentative response. "Do you live here?"

The weasel bobs and weaves from side to side like a dancing boxer. "Live where? Here? Not down that hole; no sir-ree. Don't know nothin' about that!"

"I mean around here, in this forest?"

"Who's askin'?" the creature says, continuing the boxer's dance.

"I'm Rusty. I followed the tunnels and came out here," he says, pointing at the opening. "I don't know where I am."

"Not my fault. No sir-ree; nothin' to do with me. Must have been somebody else."

"I'm not accusing you of anything. I'm going to find truth and the Castle of Love. Do you know how to get there from here?"

"Castle? Of love? Never heard of it. Don't know nothin' about no white castle."

"Who said it's white? You *do* know about it."

The weasel freezes. "Oops, did I say white? Don't know why I said that. No sir-ree. Lucky guess, I guess. Well...gotta go!"

Biting up the mouse, he disappears down the hole.

"What truth is this?" Rusty mumbles after it.

Stepping through the brush down onto the path, he eagerly scans both directions. *Hmm...I wonder which way?* Landing on the right-hand side, he begins to walk.

The Major is right, I don't know spit about life outside the castle. What dangers lurk? What if I've made a mistake? I'm all alone. I'll die!'

Leaves rustle, and a stick snaps behind him.

He spins around. *There's something out there; I can feel it.*

Unease quickens his pace.

The forested path gives way to a meadow. A small grass hut with smoke trickling from its roof sits alongside the path just up ahead.

Perhaps whoever lives there can tell me how to get to the Castle of Love.

Arriving, he traverses the campsite. A small hide of long, pure-white fur is stretched on a drying rack. On a spit over smouldering coals are the skeletal remains of a half-eaten, small carcass. He stops for a moment, feeling his stomach tighten at the sight.

Oh, Thumper...

"Hello, is there anyone here?" he calls out.

"Enter!" sounds from within.

Pulling back an animal-hide-covered shield protecting the hut's entrance, he steps in.

After a few moments, his eyes adjust to the darkness to find an Elder sitting on the edge of a grass bed, a small fire before him in the centre of the space.

His face is drooped with wrinkles. Blank yellow eyes under bushy white eyebrows stare straight ahead. Long white hair drapes down his shoulders and back. His garb is adorned with decorative patterns embroidered on the chest and sleeves. A massive eagle talon attached to a braided-hair necklace glows a deep indigo hue in the fire's light as it dangles from his neck.

The old man pats a second bed beside him. "Sit."

Rusty appreciates the comfort it provides.

"Welcome, young wanderer. Are you hungry? I have some fine rabbit to share."

"No! I couldn't possibly eat that! That would be like eating my best friend Thumper. He died."

"With every death comes a story." Elder nods his head knowingly. "Tell me."

"Thumper was my pet rabbit. Just before my father died, he built a nice cage for him to live in. One morning, I got up to feed him and found the cage empty. Something had pried the door open and there were pieces of bloodied white fur strewn everywhere inside. He was nowhere to be found."

"Loss is never easy. It is heavy to hold on to that which is gone," Elder says. The sombre pause is interrupted. "I sense you are lost. What is it you seek?"

"I've managed to get free from my horrible home, and I'm seeking truth on my way to the Castle of Love up on the other mountain. I do not know the way. Do you?"

"You already know all you need to know. Your heart already knows the road."

Rusty's brow scrunches at the words.

Reaching down, Elder feels around beside him and picks up a small pouch. "Let us steep."

After filling his cupped palm with rust-coloured powder, his teeth draw the string closed, and he sets the pouch aside.

As he slowly pours it into the fire, bright multi-coloured sparkle fills the space.

Bathed in the glitter, Rusty begins to feel tranquil and elated. A peculiar floating sensation overcomes his body, bringing with it a heightened connectedness to his surroundings. Complete relaxation brings on a bout of the giggles.

Elder reaches out and finds Rusty's knee. Deep orange eyes continue to gaze straight ahead. "You came to me in a vision many moon-sets ago, young one. In this vision I saw stags, two of them, butting heads and locking horns in a vicious battle over you. One is known as Ego. His horns point with anger, hatred, loneliness, self-doubt, shame, and struggle. The other is named Soul. His horns point with humility, faith, appreciation, empathy, confidence, and surrender." The storyteller's eyes close in silence.

Rusty waits eagerly in the lurch before impatience prevails. "What happens? Which one wins?"

Nodding alert, Elder's head bobs gently up and down knowingly. "The one you feed."

"Feed? Feed them what?"

"Hmm, good question..." His head stops in contemplation. "Temptation, surrender, and enjoyment." Smugly, Elder lies on his bed and becomes still.

Rusty stares at him, trying to make sense of it all. *What truth is this?*

Drowsy watching the flames dance to Elder's gentle snoring, he lies down into slumber.

Messenger of Love

Engulfed in a bed of thick, soft grass, Rusty wakes to the sun beaming down on the green meadow. Sitting up, he rubs his eyes and looks around in confusion. He pivots to his right. *Where's the...?* Then to his left. *And the...?* He finds himself alone, all trace of the hut and Elder vanished.

Was it all a dream?

He stretches upon standing and looks around the meadow.

I'm all alone...again. And I still don't know which way to go. He resumes his course along the path.

I already know what I need to know? I already know the road? That doesn't make any sense. How can I possibly know when I've never been here or to the Castle of Love?

The path once again becomes lined with thick brush. There is an occasional rustling of leaves behind, seeming to stop each time he does. Brisk of pace, he keeps a vigilant eye on the passing bushes around him, chased by the sense of being watched.

I see my Ego stag and how I feed it. I surrendered to the temptation of hating my life and enjoy being victim to it. I hate my home and not being allowed to do the things I want to do. I hate being lonely all the time with no friends. Yes, I feed my Ego stag often. But I don't know about this Soul stag.

"I want to fly!" A voice floats on the forest breeze.

"I vant to stay!" floats a second accent.

"Fly." "Stay." "Fly!" "Stay!"

Looking around to detect the source, Rusty spots an object about half his size dangling from a thick branch. It appears to be a huge butterfly hanging upside down with bright green wings wrapped around itself as if in a firm embrace. Its eyes are clamped shut. Chrysalis remnants lie in a pile on the ground beneath it.

It begins to squirm and wiggle vigorously. "Some... times...I feel...I could just bust out of this suffocating shell and...spread my wings and fly!" the one voice says.

Suddenly it stops and begins to smile and rock slowly back and forth. Closed eyes relax as it snuggles into its own hug. "Mmm...it's so soft and comfortable and varm inside here; so safe. I vant to stay forever," the other voice says.

All motion ceases.

"Hey there! Do you know if this path leads to the Castle of Love?" Rusty says.

Resuming its struggle, the butterfly pays him no attention. The squirming wiggle of, "I want to fly" is followed by the rocking self-embrace of, "I vant to stay" to become quiet and motionless again.

"There is no chrysalis, you know. All you have to do is open your wings and you can fly away," Rusty notes.

Again, there is no reply before the struggle and banter renews. The butterfly is too self-absorbed in its debate to notice Rusty's presence.

He carries on down the path. *What truth is this?*

Glimpsing movement in the thick brush up ahead, his pace stalls as he tries to make out the source.

Life freezes when a wolf lands on the path in front of him.

Hunched down, the predator begins a slow, grumbling circle of its prey.

"What do you want?" Rusty turns slowly to match it.

"You travel alone, like me, a lone wolf going your own way," the wolf growls at him.

"Who are you?" Rusty says.

"Yes, I know you, engaging in only forced connection with your pack. Yes, a lone wolf."

"What do you want?"

"You want to be alone...no, you *need* to be alone." The wolf snaps teeth at him.

"That's not true. I'm going to have lots of friends at the Castle of Love."

"Look around; you have no place with others. You live alone and you will die alone!"

A barking lunge at him causes Rusty to cringe and recoil.

"I'm not afraid of you," Rusty offers as a weak defense.

Howling to the sky, the wolf sets to strike.

Rusty raises his arm to shield himself.

A sudden, high-pitched whistle pierces the moment.

The wolf draws back at the shrill sound to hunch down, its steely-grey eyes fixed on something beyond its prey.

Half turning, Rusty sees a man atop a unicorn. He is dressed in pink lingerie and a large-brimmed pink hat with a white feather pluming out back from its band.

With head down and one hoof scraping at the ground, the unicorn's sights are locked on the wolf. The blasting whistle coming from its peculiar phallic-shaped horn abruptly stops...the shrillness lingering in the hushed forest.

"To silence the wolf, I invite you to feel your fear young man. Feel that fear...feel every bit of it," the man says.

Trembling, Rusty looks back at the snarling wolf's attention locked on a new opponent.

"It is yourself that you are afraid of, not the wolf. Feel it! Love it! Love the way it feels."

"I'm so scared!" Rusty's tears erupt. "I'm scared of this wolf. I'm scared to be out here, lost and alone. I'm scared of the world outside. I'm scared I will die."

"Golden! That's the way!" the man cheers.

As Rusty's tears subside, he notices the tension has eased. The wolf is sitting quietly, looking at him, its inquisitive head cocked to one side. The unicorn is grazing on some grass while the man, dismounted, is standing with a comforting hand on his shoulder.

"Reach out your hand to the wolf," the man leans in with a whisper.

Wiping away his tears, a hesitant Rusty looks to the man and then with trepidation to the wolf.

"Go ahead, try it." The man gestures forward.

Rusty stretches out the back of his hand toward the wolf.

Sniffing the air, the wolf tentatively moves toward it until its nose touches. Rusty flinches at the cool wetness. He tries stroking the wolf's nose and is startled when the wolf responds by licking his hand. Slowly, he moves to pet its head. It sidles up tightly against him. All reluctance evaporates as he vigorously rubs the furry neck behind its ears. The wolf pulls away to bounce about, tail wagging while darting at Rusty's hands and then away.

Rusty starts to laugh and chase after to touch the wolf.

The game continues for several moments when, abruptly, the wolf bounds off toward the bushes. It stops for one final look back at the boy before disappearing into the brush.

Rusty gives a silent wave of goodbye. *What truth is this?* "That was amazing! Who are you?" he says, turning to the man.

"I am Pink Knighty, a Messenger of the First Order of Love, at your service," he says, removing his hat to take a deep bow. "And this is my most honoured steed, Dicky."

The unicorn rears and whistles a short note.

"I have never seen a knight like you before. You dress weird."

"I am a special kind of knight. I was bestowed the unique name and uniform after I expanded the collective honeycomb with my discovery of the Femman inside of me. The uniform is worn as a symbol to honour this aspect of my nature. The title of Knighty was created to distinguish a particular order of the knighthood that acts to honour my discovery."

"What is the collective honeycomb?" Rusty says.

"Every living thing has a honeycomb of love through which the light of its Soul-Source shines. The more we discover about ourselves, the larger grows our honeycomb and the more connected we are to Soul-Source. Because we are all connected, our honeycombs connect, bringing together the individual souls to form the greater collective consciousness of love, of Soul-Source."

"Do I have a honeycomb of love?"

"Absolutely! However, I sense yours is fairly small for one your age. Your growth has been stunted. I also sense many of your cells blocked by pain. Your soul has been wounded; consumed by blackness. Those cells need to be flushed in order to heal."

"How do I flush my wounded cells, Knighty?"

"As you have just flushed one - by feeling your feelings - fully...completely. Whenever we judge a feeling, we block it from flowing and shut down that cell. Feelings are energy, and energy is meant to flow. They are simply feelings and nothing to be afraid of. Release your judgement and feel the feelings that create the blockage and you will flush."

Rusty contemplates Knighty's words.

"You said that you are lost; from where?"

"I'm walking away from my horrible life in search of truth on my way to the Castle of Love. I don't know the way and I'm lost. Do you know how to get there?"

"Yes. I know this castle well. You are on the right path."

"Can you take me there?"

"Oh no, your journey to the Castle of Love must be travelled alone my friend, it is the only way. What I can offer is to come to your aid should you ever find yourself in need of my services."

Lifting the pink sequined flap of the white man-purse slung over his shoulder, Knighty pulls out a necklace dangling a small whistle the shape of the unicorn's horn. "Just blow this and I will find you."

Rusty receives the phallic whistle with disgust.

Mounting his steed, Knighty puts fists to hips. "As we say in the Order, be knighty, my friend." He tips his hat and the pair trots off down the path in the opposite direction to Rusty's travel.

Rusty contemplates the whistle before draping it around his neck and resuming his journey. *What truth is this?*

GREAT COMFORT

Standing on the edge of a high embankment looking down into a valley at a distant river, Rusty can see a fork in the path at the bottom of the hill. A shorter leg leads to a wide crossing. The much longer leg leads to a suspension bridge over the narrowest point where the river converges into a raging gorge.

As he makes his way down the hill, the weather turns cloudy grey. The wind picks up, and a chill overtakes him.

Stopping at the fork, he reads the top sign on the post: *Lonely River – cross at your own peril.*

Beneath it is a second sign in the shape of an arrow pointing down one of the legs, reading, *Bridge.*

Beneath it, a third sign pivots around erratically with the wind. Turning the arrow upright, he reads *Shortcut* pointing down the other leg. His eagerness opts for the shorter route.

Arriving on the bank, he ponders the flooded crossing as rain begins to pelt down.

I'll wash away in that. No crossing here.

Hypnotized by watching the river run, a profound loneliness consumes him.

Feel it! Love it! Love the way it feels, echoes.

I'm all alone...lost and alone. Whimpering, he hangs his head. *I want somebody to be with me. I want somebody to love. But there's nobody, just me...all alone...all...a...lone. The emptiness inside...nobody wants me.* "Somebody love me, please!" he cries out skyward.

An attempt at skipping a small stone fails miserably.

Why would you, though? I'm not worth it...I'm not worth it. I'm just a nobody. I have nothing to offer...nothing. Who am I, anyways? Just a nobody...all alone.

"Well, I don't need you!" He stamps his foot on the ground. "I don't need anybody! Just me...just me."

The wolf's words flooding back strike him with revelation. *I AM a lone wolf. I'm most at peace on my own. I draw comfort from it, from within me. When loneliness creeps in, I look outside myself but never find comfort. Seems if I don't go within, I go without. It's not being alone that hurts; it's being lonely. There's a big difference between those two.*

Befuddled by a river level suddenly passable, he scans for the best route across.

On the opposite bank, sunshine beaming through a small portal in the clouds spotlights a child dressed in a frilly white lace dress and wide-brimmed white sun hat sitting in the glow. Seemingly unaware of the miserable surrounding conditions, she is playing with the flowers.

Looking to him, the child's face is obscured by long curly locks of orange hair and the drooping brim of the hat.

What a beautiful sight; so peaceful and innocent.

Awareness hits him.

I can't cross here. My suffering risks forever corrupting that sweet, innocent child's world by introducing suffering's very existence. I can't do that to her.

Turning back, he takes the much longer route to a suspension bridge swaying and jerking in the gusty wind. The violent white river roars as it fights to push through the narrow gorge far below. Cold and wet, the traveller clutches the slippery rope railings and begins his treacherous passage.

Several steps in, a voice calls out. "Who goes there?"

A sack swings up from underneath to land heavily in Rusty's path, followed by a troll clambering up after it.

Standing a scrawny four feet tall on big, callused feet, its creviced face is covered by a shaggy, matted beard, and big ears poke out from wild, matted hair. A large, hairy mole protrudes from the tip of a long, beak-like nose. It rubs grimy, crooked fingers down tattered, filthy clothing while its two beady, bloodshot eyes stare Rusty up and down. The stench is repulsive.

Heaving up the sack and slinging it over its left shoulder, it hunches forward to support the weight.

"No one crosses my bridge without payment! Pay or perish!"

Nervously looking over the side at the raging river below, Rusty responds, "But I have no money."

"Money?" The troll breaks into cackling laughter. "Who needs money? I gave that up years ago."

"Then what do you want?"

"Rocks!" Its brow rises in anticipation.

"Rocks?" Rusty snickers. "What do you want rocks for?"

"To put in my sack." It twists to point at the load resting on its back.

"Why do you carry a sack of rocks?"

"Because it is of much value to me. The burden gives me great comfort."

"Any particular kind of rocks?"

"Yours!"

"But I don't have any rocks either."

"Well, you best be getting yourself some, now, shouldn't you?"

As Rusty backs up to search the river bank for some currency, the troll calls after him, "Get heavy ones; the heavier, the better."

There are plenty of rocks to be had. He picks up a couple to serve as payment and returns.

"Will these do?"

"Perfect!" The troll stomps about, howling with glee. "Now, throw each one at me with an insult."

Rusty's head tilts with scrunched eyebrows.

"Go on, hit me with your best shot," the troll says.

"Alright, you're ugly!" The first rock strikes the troll in the chest before falling to the bridge deck.

"Perfect!" It claps.

"And you stink!" The second stone strikes the troll between the eyes before it too falls to the deck.

"Perfect!" The troll howls with glee as it drops the sack in front and opens it. Picking up the first installment of Rusty's payment, it mumbles, "Ugly," while stroking it on the way to being gently placed inside. "Stinky" is then picked up and placed.

Standing mesmerized by the apparent beauty of the contents, the troll slowly rubs its hands together and licks its lips in anticipation.

"May I cross now?"

There is no response from the troll, spellbound by the sight.

Rusty hears "Friends" murmured as he gingerly side-steps the troll and sack.

Crossing the remainder of the bridge, he reconnects with the path on the other side of the gorge. Looking back, he sees the troll still standing there in a trance.

What truth is this? Nose forward, he resumes his journey.

The troll suddenly looks around suspiciously. Closing up the sack, it climbs over the side and under the bridge. A gangly arm reaches up from underneath, and the sack vanishes.

MASQUERADE OF MIRRORS

The trees have become sparse, and the soil, now rust-red in colour, sparkles in the bright sun. Standing tall, the flat-topped outcroppings of red stone dot the terrain. The rocky-rough path runs along a creek, winding its way through the red hills.

Rusty encounters a lone, horse-drawn carnival wagon parked in a clearing beside the path. The side is brightly coloured with the words *Masquerade of Mirrors* painted in large script. There are steps on the back leading up to a small closed door. A mule, tethered to a rope suspended between two trees, is quietly grazing in behind.

"A carnival?! I've always wanted to go to the carnival," he blurts, running up to it.

No one appears to be around.

"Hello...? Hello...?"

There is no answer. He ascends the steps to the back door, over which a sign reads, *All the world is your mirror.*

"Hello?"

Again, there is no reply.

A knock on the door causes it to creak wide open.

The light streaming in reveals Rusty's long shadow stretching up heavy velvet, burgundy curtains lining the walls of an empty space.

He pokes his head in.

"Hello...?"

With no reply, he climbs inside.

Suddenly, the door slams shut and he is immersed in total darkness. Frantic, he grapples for an exit no longer there, having been replaced by soft, velvety fabric.

"Hey, pecker-head," a creepy voice says.

"Who's there?" Rusty's panicked reach to touch something is met by nothing but air.

A large oval mirror illuminates in front of him, reflecting his elongated self. Wavy body stretched tall, he begins to chuckle at his long limbs as he wiggles them like wet noodles.

The mirror darkens, and an identical one lights up to the left of it. Stepping in front, his image is now squashed short. He giggles at the stubby limbs as he stomps his fat feet and swings his pudgy arms in a marching motion.

When the mirror darkens, another lights up to his left, and he steps in front it with excited anticipation. His shape normal, the reflection is downtrodden, and looking at him pleadingly, cheeks wet with tears.

Cringing, Rusty looks away.

"Mwa-ha-ha," the sinister voice cackles as the mirror darkens and the next one illuminates.

Reluctantly, he steps left in front of it, the next of many, each a step to his left.

The gopher foraging for food panics upon seeing Rusty and flees down its hole, leaving the scene abandoned; Major Rajor, contorted in furious anguish, shakes his fist at Rusty; the weasel taps paws against chest as if to say, "Not me!" before bobbing and weaving in the boxer's dance and turning its back to hide behind itself; Elder's green eyes stare off into the distance, the pouch dangling at his side in one hand while the outstretched other points the way; the butterfly, eyes clamped shut, struggles in its own embrace.

"Mwa-ha-ha-ha-ha...."

The lone wolf silhouetted in a bright, yellow moon howls at the sky; Pink Knighty rears on Dicky with hat-in-hand thrust into the air. Rusty clutches at the whistle dangling around his neck. The little girl's peaceful innocence shocks him when it is his face framed in the long locks of curly orange hair; the troll struggles under the weight of the bulging sack slung over his shoulder, peering up with a look of feigned enjoyment.

Suddenly, all of the mirrors light up and surround Rusty with illuminated ovals. He spins around, confused, confronted by all of the characters.

"They are but you masquerading as them," the menacing voice groans before breaking into a full-on evil guffaw.

All the mirrors abruptly extinguish, leaving the room in a dead black silence.

The door creaks as it opens, allowing daylight to flood into the empty space.

Squinting at the glare, Rusty scrambles out the door and down the steps. The door slams shut behind him.

He hastens down the path while looking back at the wagon in confusion.

What truth is this?

No One is Coming

What's with those mirrors? And that sign over the door — All the world is your mirror?

An eagle's distinctive screech soaring high above calls to all below. Rusty stops and looks up.

How majestic. Aw, to be so powerful...and so free....

Resuming his walk, he mimics the sinister voice: "They are but you masquerading as them."

So they're me in disguise? I'm them and they're me? I'm a sorrowful, angry, confused, lonely little girly-boy who's afraid of his own shadow?

The resonance in the words drills to the very core of his being.

I don't like me one bit. His head hangs, and he kicks a pebble along the way.

Rounding a curve in the path, he finds a huge eagle sitting on a stump as if waiting for him. The captivating sight stalls him in his step.

Its white head with hooked yellow beak jerks randomly as its attention flits from one focal point to another. Rugged yellow feet with sharp indigo talons click and scratch on the wood as it sets about adjusting the position of its massive black body.

The great bird cocks its head and squawks, "Why so sad?"

"I've left my terrible home in search of truth and the Castle of Love. It's been a long, tiring journey, and I've just learned the truth about what kind of a person I am, and I don't like what I've found."

"And what truth is this?" The eagle fidgets.

"I'm ugly! I'm scared and angry and lonely and a femme."

"So why is that a bad thing?"

"Because I don't want to be like that."

"But you are. Why not embrace it?"

Staring into the piercing black pupils within crystalline white eyes, Rusty becomes mesmerized and loses all sense of his surroundings.

"When I was a chick, I clung to the sanctuary of my nest and the protection of Mother."

As if seeing the world through the eagle's eyes, Rusty experiences being alone and huddled in a nest high up, gazing at open sky.

"As I grew, I wanted to fly, but I was afraid to try. I felt ashamed: a useless eagle unworthy of flight."

Shame washes over Rusty as he quivers. Mother swoops in to land on the edge, dropping fresh kill for him.

"Only you can take the leap of faith that you will fly. No one is coming to do that for you," Mother says down to him. "Acknowledge your fear and shame and accept in your heart that you are that way. Once you embrace those aspects of who you truly are, you will discover the courage to fly."

Pushing off, she glides up to the highest point on the tree to oversee a world at her disposal.

"I remember the day I felt ready to jump." The eagle's words stoop Rusty back to be present in the moment. "It was sheer terror as I stepped to the edge and looked down at the nothingness between me and the ground below. Gulping for courage, I pushed off, panicking as I flapped helplessly toward the ground. When the air caught and suspended me on the updraft, I flapped my wings and soared. Oh, the joy and worthiness I felt as I claimed my birthright."

The eagle flexes its wings as it stands up. "Make no mistake, as old and as wise as I have become, I still catch myself afraid and ashamed. Embrace who you are, and you too will soar."

Spreading its gigantic wings and pushing off with a flapping breeze, the great bird circles overhead with a loud screech.

He watches as it disappears over an outcropping. *What truth is this?*

Resuming his journey, he reflects on the wisdom the eagle shared.

I acknowledge my ugliness, but I sure don't accept it, let alone embrace who I am. It's really quite simple. I am who I am, that's who I am. Who's to love me? Me, that's who; no one is coming. I will love me for who I am.

As he smiles with eyes closed, his imaginary wings wrap around him. "I love you Rusty," he says while gently squeezing a warm embrace.

His arms open to full spread in the afternoon sun streaming down on him, warm and welcoming.

A PATH

Rusty takes a deep whiff. *I love the solitude and serenity of it all; that sense of connectedness. Being in nature is so amazing.*

Lost in thought, Rusty is startled and dodges another person walking a different path merging with his onto a field of flowers.

A woman stands before him dressed in a royal blue, loose-fitting silky shirt and matching pants. Tied around her waist is a black sash with a rainbow embroidered on one end. Her blonde hair is pulled back in a tight, short ponytail.

Their eyes lock. Her sky-blue gaze is observant yet intriguingly inviting.

A warm smile creases her face. "Hello, friend. I am Princess. Who are you?"

"I'm Rusty."

"It is a gift to meet you." She offers a clasped-handed, shallow bow.

"Can you tell me if this path leads to the Castle of Love?"

"This depends which Castle of Love you seek. Every path leads to one. What you find depends on what you look for."

"It's the one on the other mountain from mine. Does this path lead there?"

"Do you wish it to?"

"Yes."

"Then it's possible it shall."

Rusty considers the prospect with perplexed interest. "Are you seeking a Castle of Love?"

"I am. I always return to one after a Tazenamy quest."

"A Tazenamy quest?" He scrunches his face.

"Yes. I go on one whenever somebody violates my boundaries. Tazenamy is my protector spirit. I invite her presence to overtake my being whenever I experience someone violating my sacred space. One's vulnerabilities are to be protected and only shared with the trusted. Once Tazenamy undertakes a quest, it must be completed with the perpetrator kicked out. This last one was particularly painful because the evicted was someone I had trusted in my space but who tried to force me off my path onto his."

"What are you the Princess of?"

"I am a Princess of the Positive Arc of Possibility."

"The Positive Arc of Possibility? Where's that?"

"It is not a place. It is a way of being; a way to travel your journey by leading with love and light. It is a way where anything is possible; where the future is held in wonder, not worry; where there is celebration in all that is right with the world. Once mastered, to travel in this manner brings spiritual nobility."

"What truth is this? Is this it, or is it the others?" Rusty says.

"Possibly, what do you mean? Truth is only so in the eyes of its beholder."

"I've learned there are other ways. Like the way of the Ego and Soul stags battling inside of me to be fed."

"That is one possible truth."

"Or flushing my wounded honeycomb of love."

"That is another possibility."

"Or to masquerade with my mirrors."

"Yet another!" she says with rising excitement.

"Or am I to acknowledge, accept, and embrace myself?"

"Still another!" she exclaims gleefully. "And there is even more possibility. Imagine if any, or all of it were the truth. Or…none of it. What if there is something more we haven't even discovered yet? How exciting is that?!"

Princess's jubilation is contagious, and Rusty begins to fidget in delight.

Taking his hands in hers, she looks him in the eye. "Hold open the door to possibility so possibility has some place to go, and you will always have a positive path to follow."

"Brilliant! I see a whole new way, a path of positive orientation."

"I appreciate you, Rusty. Not everyone is capable of grasping the Arc so readily. And I honour you. I appreciate the courage it takes for one to seek their Castle of Love."

"Aw, it's no big deal." He squirms shyly.

"Oh, but it is! Appreciate being appreciated, Rusty. You are significant. I am honoured to walk with you."

"Thank you, Princess," he says humbly. "You seem like you have been travelling this path for a long time."

"A few season-cycles now. For much of my time, I cared for my children, and now that they are grown, I have set out to start a new life on my own. My heart hears a calling; of lending a helping hand some place; of saving kangaroos, as I like to say. There have been many good-byes and along with them many tears."

"What do you hope to find at your Castle of Love, Princess?"

"I seek spending my summers in the sun, painting seashells by the seashore. And what do you hope to find at yours, Rusty?"

"I hold open the possibility that I'll find it all...the truth...and more!" His dramatization causes them both to burst into laughter.

"I'm most grateful for you coming into my life, Princess. I have a strong temptation to love you, and as I surrender to the feeling, I experience enjoyment. You've helped me find my Soul stag!"

Princess smiles and, swinging hand-in-hand, the two stroll off, blissfully immersed in the pleasure of each other's company.

Peaceful on His Shoulder

Having appeared through the forest, the white-stone wall now towers in front of Rusty and Princess. Fingertips on the end of his outstretched arm glide over the rough surface.

"Can it be? Can this be my Castle of Love? Let's find the entrance."

Taking off with Princess following in close pursuit, he runs along the wall, stopping at a large wooden door with *LOVE LIVES HERE* declared in the carved header. The engraved words individually stained in the planks please the eye: *peace, joy, harmony, gratitude, appreciation, empathy, and compassion.*

"This must be it!" he says.

Trying the latch, he finds it unlocked. With a slight push, the heavy door opens effortlessly. Rushing through immerses him in a beautiful courtyard. Bushes lining the castle walls are meticulously manicured into various animal shapes. Polished cobblestone walkways separate lush flowerbeds with countless butterflies flittering about. Bird songs float on moist air while hummingbirds dart about the garden.

A magnificent fountain occupies the middle of the grounds. The large, white, carved-stone centrepiece statue is a toga-clad female figure with leaf crown. She is pouring water from a large urn held in her arms. Splashing down onto her feet, water finds its way into the pond base abundant with fish.

Familiarity haunts him. *This fountain is like the one from my old castle; only this one is alive.*

Suspiciously scanning for the staircase leading up to the rampart, he finds the bramble bush at the base of the stairs gone, replaced by a beautiful flowerbed surrounding a massive rock placed where the sinkhole was located.

Faint remnants of engraved words fall underfoot as he races up the weathered stone steps.

Looking to the other mountain where the Castle of Love stood, there is nothing but trees, hills, and mountains. A tiny eagle soars high above distant trees. Confused, he descends the stairs.

What truth is this? This can't be the same castle. I would have seen the door.

Looking over reveals the possibility that it was shrouded by the huge bush now trimmed into an arched doorway trellis, the bench having been moved to a new location.

Sitting down on the polished marble of the fountain's base, his hands smack his face at epiphany's strike.

"There was no other Castle! The truth is I've always lived in the Castle of Love."

Relief trickles tears of joy down his cheeks.

"Welcome home, Rusty; welcome home," Princess's loving voice caresses him.

A butterfly flutters up and lands, peaceful on his shoulder.

The Beginning

Made in the USA
Monee, IL
01 June 2021

69217764R10028